This book belongs to:

_____

Le Beestro

Honey Due Mellon.................$10.00
Honey Mustard Viniagrette.....$10.00
Honey Combs........................$10.00
Honey Tea, with Honey..........$10.00
Spam and Honey....................$10.00
Honeyed Ham.......................$10.00
Honey Bunches of Oats...........$10.00
Honey Glazed Carrots.............$10.00
Ambrosia.............................$10.00
Bread & Honey......................$10.00
Honey Nut Cheerios...............$10.00
Honey Sticks.........................$10.00
Honey Dew Juice...................$10.00
Honey Mead.........................$10.00
Nectar N' Honey....................$10.00

Bug Your Mom Day

Miss Spider's Sunny Patch Friends

Bug Your Mom Day

David Kirk

CALLAWAY

NEW YORK

2008

It was Bug Your Mom Day in Sunny Patch, a day when bugs show their moms how much they love them.

Miss Spider was taking her mom, Betty Beetle, to lunch at Le Beestro.

Holley decided to surprise her by tidying the house.

"**I**'m going to make Mom the best Bug Your Mom Day gift ever!" announced Dragon excitedly.

"*No!*" insisted Squirt. "Mine will be the best!"

"No, *mine!*" the other kids chimed in, one after the other.

The only bug who didn't argue was Wiggle, who said simply, "I am going to make Mom a card."

The other kids giggled. A card? That wasn't nearly enough for the best mom in Sunny Patch!

The kids flew, hopped, and skittered out the door to look for the perfect gift for Miss Spider.

Pansy, Snowdrop, and Shimmer gathered big bunches of violets and forget-me-nots.

Dragon looked for the muddiest mud so that Miss Spider could have a mud bath.

Spinner collected beautiful seed pods. Squirt found Miss Spider a pea pod dish rack. Bounce went to the Dribbly Dell.

"Berry for Mommy!" he shouted, landing on his favorite bush. "Bigger!" he bellowed, bouncing to another, bigger berry.

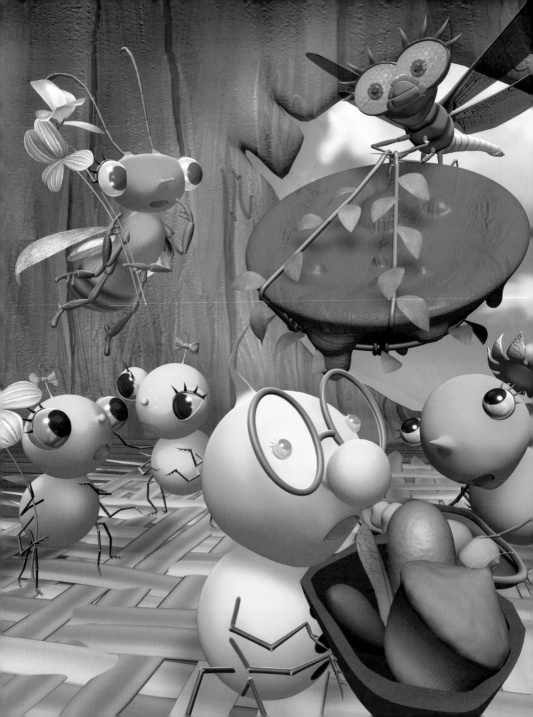

B

ack home, the little bugs argued over whose gift was the best.

"Forget all that stuff! Look what I found!" yelled Dragon, bursting through the door with his tub of mucky mud.

Crash! The gifts were shattered! The house was splattered! Holley was not happy.

Neither were the little bugs—their gifts were ruined!

Wiggle offered his leaf. "My card is dry. We can say it's from all of us."

Nobody liked Wiggle's idea. His card was puny and plain. They knew they could do much better.

Spinner spun a new card. All the kids decorated it with violets, daisies, daffodils, dewdrops, and berries. When they were finished, Bounce came bouncing in rolling an *extra* fat, extra squishy jumbo blueberry!

"Bounce! No!" everybuggy screamed.

It was too late. *Sploosh!* Sticky blueberry juice splashed everywhere.

just then, Miss Spider came home.

"Oh my!" she exclaimed.

"We were trying to make you a super-spiderific Bug Your Mom Day gift," Squirt sighed.

W iggle crept up shyly behind his mother.

"But here is a little card from all of us," he said.

"Why, Wiggle, this is beautiful!" beamed Miss Spider.

"**B**ut the very best Bug Your Mom Day gift of all is knowing how much my darlings love me."

This book is based on the TV episode "Bug Your Mom Day," written by Steven Sullivan,
from the animated TV series *Miss Spider's Sunny Patch Friends* on Nick Jr.,
a Nelvana Limited/Absolute Pictures Limited co-production in association with
Callaway Arts & Entertainment, based on the Miss Spider books by David Kirk.

Digital art by Callaway Animation Studios under the direction of David Kirk
in collaboration with Nelvana Limited.

ISBN 978-0-448-45025-4   10 9 8 7 6 5 4 3 2 1

ABOUT DAVID KIRK

Master artist and storyteller David Kirk is hailed as one of today's most innovative and exciting creators of books and toys for children. Before his remarkable success in the world of children's publishing, Kirk was the founder and designer of two toy companies. His bright, hand-painted wooden toys are, together with his paintings and hand-crafted furniture, treasured by collectors and featured in books, art galleries, and museums.

Then along came a spider: Miss Spider. Inspired by his daughter Violet's love for insects in the family garden, Kirk found the perfect subject for his story. *Miss Spider's Tea Party,* a lush counting book in verse with mesmerizing oil illustrations and an important message about tolerance, quickly became a phenomenon, earning praise from booksellers and librarians across the country. Kirk followed this success by continuing the saga of Miss Spider in *Miss Spider's Wedding, Miss Spider's New Car,* and *Miss Spider's ABC.*

In addition to creating splendid books and paintings, Mr. Kirk finds time to develop his many other projects, including designing Sunny Patch, a collection of children's lifestyle products, for Target stores. He is also executive producer of *Miss Spider's Sunny Patch Friends,* a 3-D computer-animated television series on Nick Jr. The success of the series inspired a line of trade and mass-market books published by Callaway Arts & Entertainment and Penguin Young Readers Group.

Mr. Kirk lives in upstate New York with his wife, Kathy, and daughters, Violet, Primrose, and Wisteria.